HOW THE MOUSE GOT BROWN TEETH

A CREE STORY FOR CHILDREN

HOW THE MOUSE GOT BROWN TEETH

A CREE STORY FOR CHILDREN

illustrated by George Littlechild
translated and edited by Freda Ahenakew

Fifth House
Saskatoon, Saskatchewan
1988

Canadian Cataloguing in Publication Data

Main entry under title:

How the mouse got brown teeth

   ISBN 0-920079-40-7

1. Cree Indians – Legends – Juvenile literature.
2. Indians of North America – Canada – Legends – Juvenile literature.
3. Legends – Canada – Juvenile literature.
4. Mice – Folklore – Juvenile literature.
I. Saskatchewan Indian Languages Institute.

E99.C88H69 1988   j398.2'08997   C88-098081-8

Special thanks to Freda Ahenakew for her invaluable assistance.

This book has been published with the assistance of:

Saskatchewan Arts Board
Canada Council

Published by

Fifth House
Suite One
128 Second Avenue N
Saskatoon, Saskatchewan
Canada S7K 2B2

Typeset by

Apex Graphics
Saskatoon, Saskatchewan

Cover design: Robert Grey

Printed in
Hong Kong by
Book Art Inc.
Toronto

Preface

This is a student story which was written in an intermediate Cree course at Saskatoon during the summer of 1982; we are grateful to Ray Smith for permission to edit and publish his work. This story was originally published in **kiskinahamawakan-acimowinisa** / **Student Stories** (Written by Cree-Speaking Students, Edited, Translated and with a Glossary by Freda Ahenakew, *Algonquian and Iroquoian Linguistics, Memoir 2,* Winnipeg 1986).

In the interest of the students who will work with the Cree version of the story, the writing has been standardized to represent the sounds of a single variant of Plains Cree — the central Saskatchewan dialect spoken on the **atahk-akohp** reserve.

This book has been prepared with the help and support of George Littlechild, who did the illustrations, and of Caroline Heath, who recognizes the need for publishing Cree legends for all children.

Since this is a traditional story, which is collectively owned by the Cree Indian people, the royalties from the sale of this book go to the Saskatchewan Indian Languages Institute.

Once there was a boy who lived with his grandmother.

"Never climb trees. You will fall and get hurt," his grandmother

told him as she left in a boat to check her nets.

The boy went into the woods to shoot arrows.

When he saw a squirrel up in a tree, he took a shot at it.

The arrow missed the squirrel and got caught in the tree.

The squirrel ran down the tree and away.

The boy started to climb the tree to get his arrow back.

He kept blowing at the arrow, trying to make it come loose.

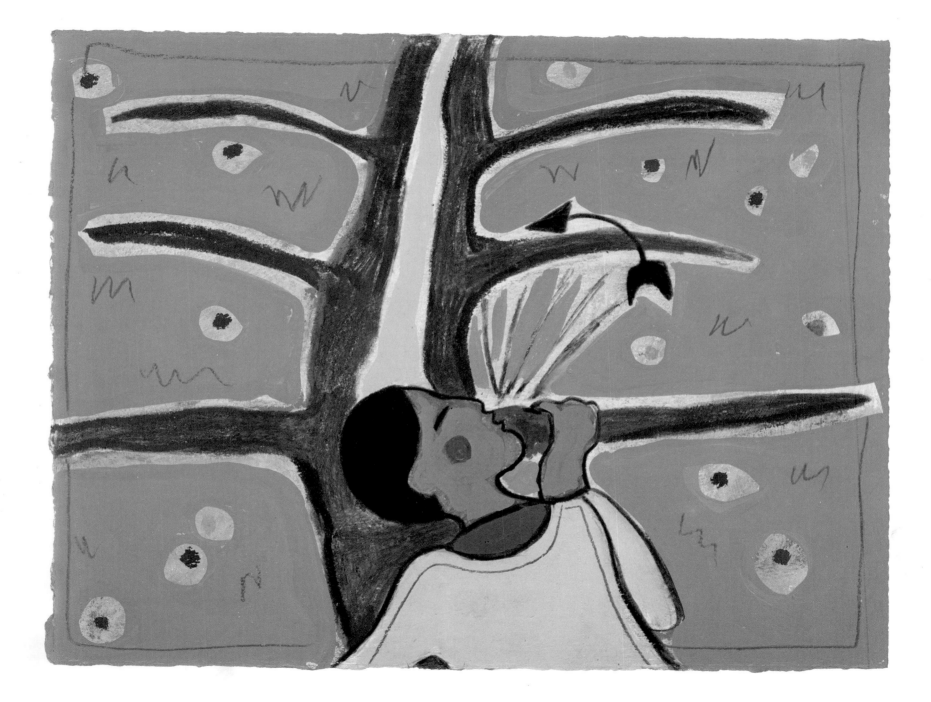

The boy had climbed high up the tree when suddenly he saw a path.

"I wonder whose path this is?" the boy thought.

"I think I'll set a snare," he said.

And so he set a snare.

When he had set the snare, he went home.

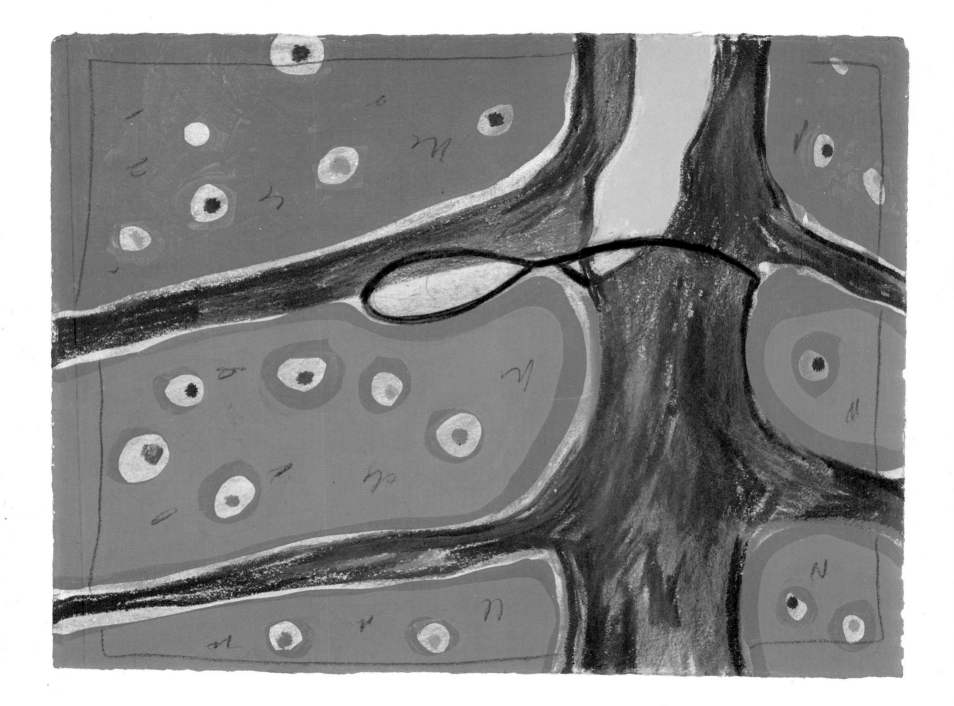

"It is getting dark," his grandmother said when she got home.

"It is time for us to go to bed soon."

And so they went to bed.

Finally the old lady had had enough sleep and she got up,
but the sun was not up yet. She woke the boy.

"Get up!" she said.
"The sun should be up and it isn't. What have you been up to?"

The boy remembered his snare and jumped out of bed.

He ran to the tree he had climbed, to check his snare.
There, caught in his snare, was the sun.

"I must help it," thought the boy.

The boy went through the woods, gathering all the animals to take back to the tree.

He hoped that one of them would be able to bite

through the snare.

One at a time he threw the animals up to try to bite through his snare.

But none of the animals was able to do it.

Finally

only the mouse was left.

The mouse ran up the tree to help the sun.

It chewed

                        and chewed

                                    and suddenly

it bit through the snare and the sun escaped.

But the little mouse fell to the ground and for a long time
lay on the road without moving.

The little boy blew and blew on the mouse to try to bring it back to life.

At last the mouse opened its eyes.   And its mouth.

That's when the boy saw that the mouse had burned its front teeth,
trying to free the sun.

And that's why, even to this day, the mouse has brown teeth.